Let's Play Ball

written by Pam Holden
illustrated by Philip Webb

We like to throw balls.

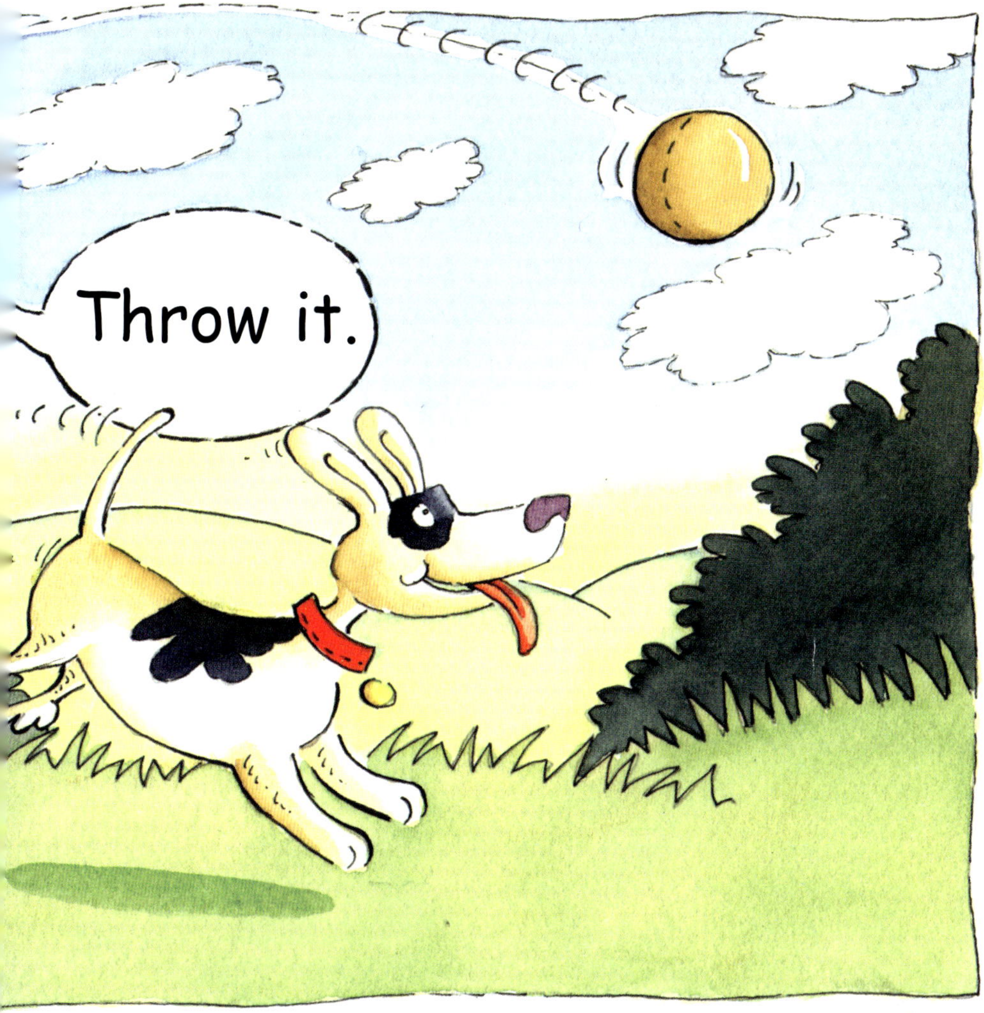
Throw it.

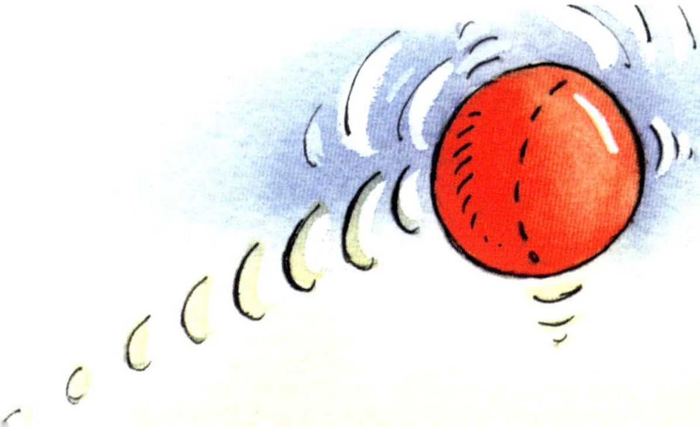

We like to hit balls.

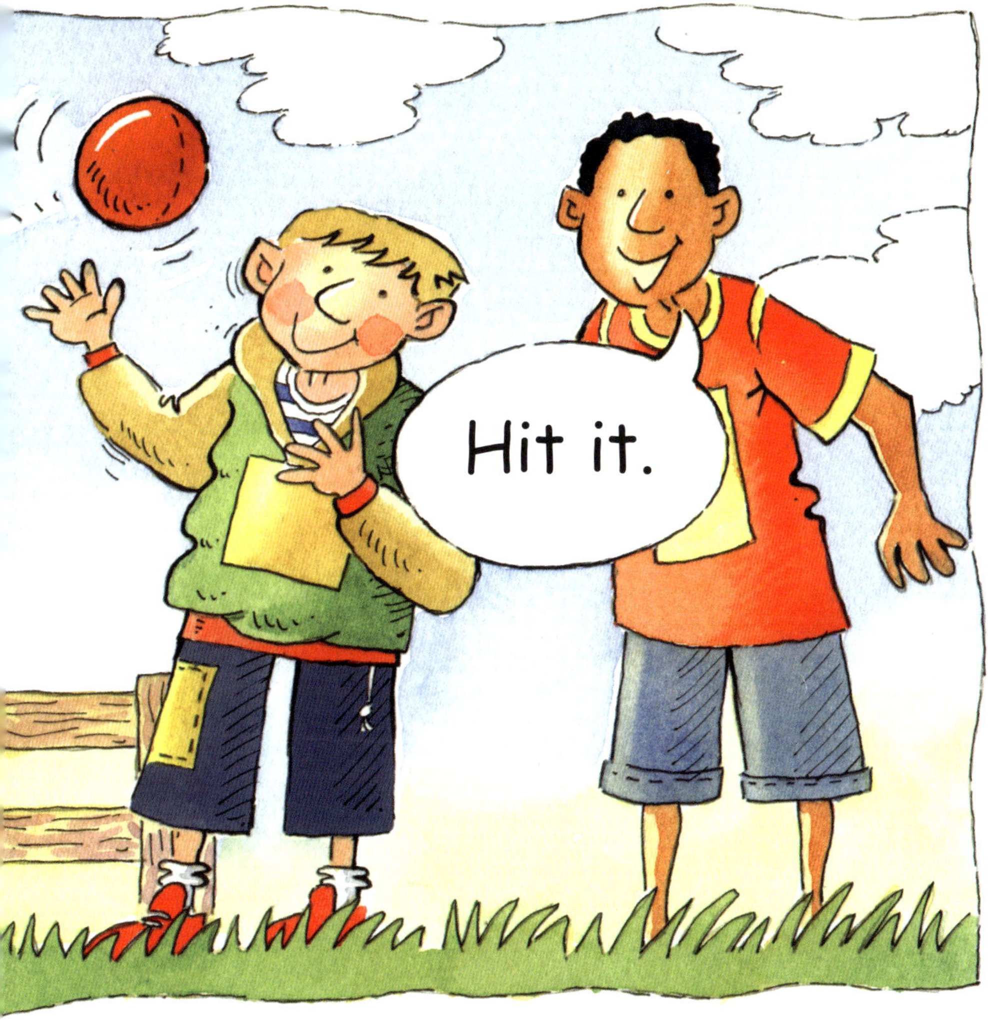
Hit it.

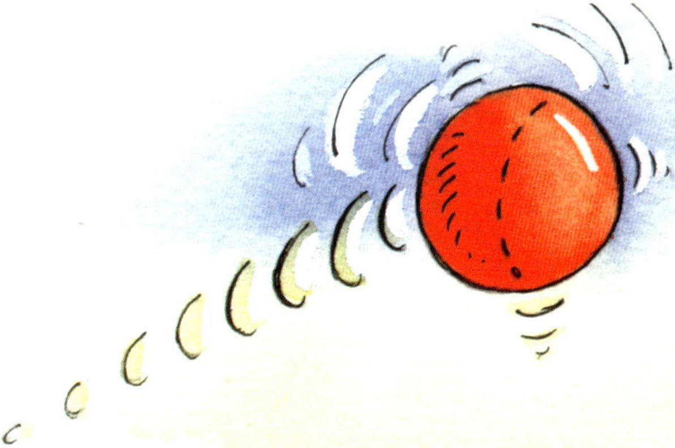

We like to kick balls.

Kick it.

We like to bounce balls.

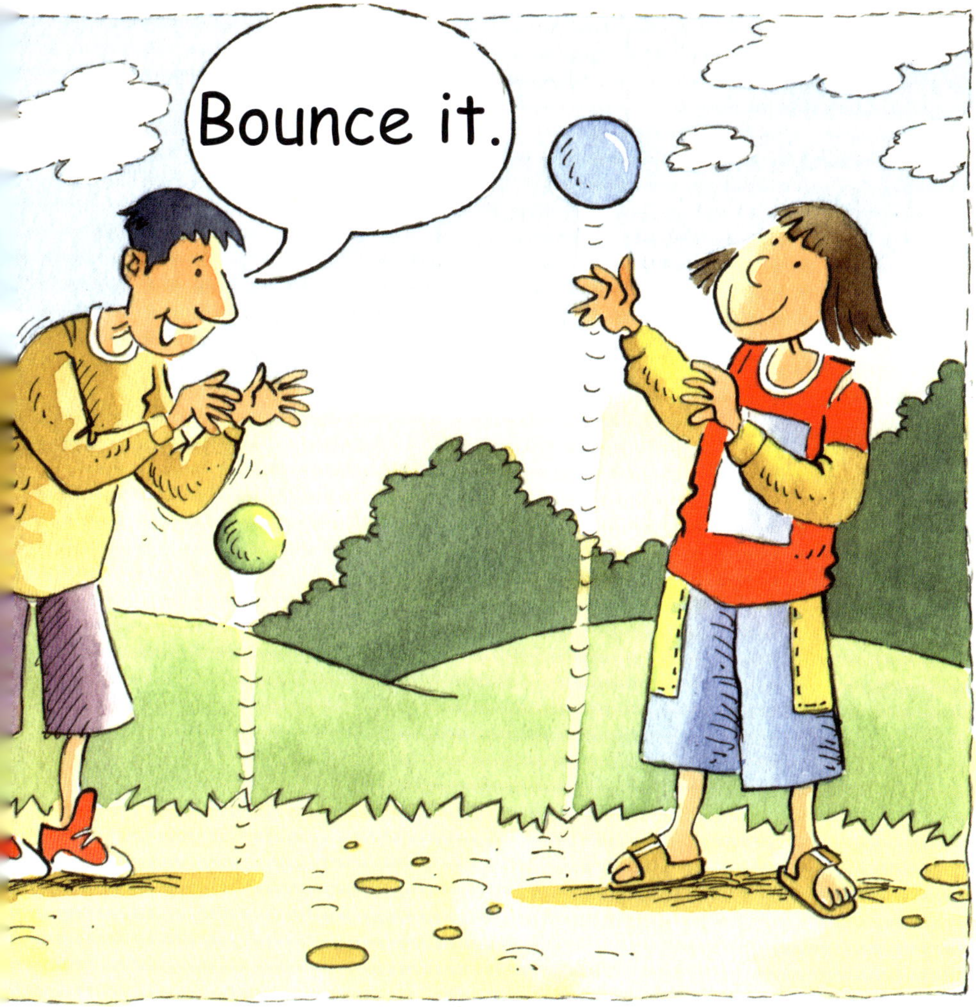
Bounce it.

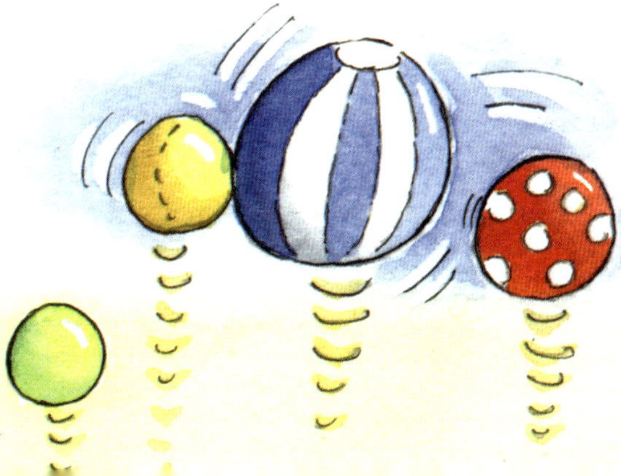

We like to bowl balls.

Bowl it.

We like to catch balls.

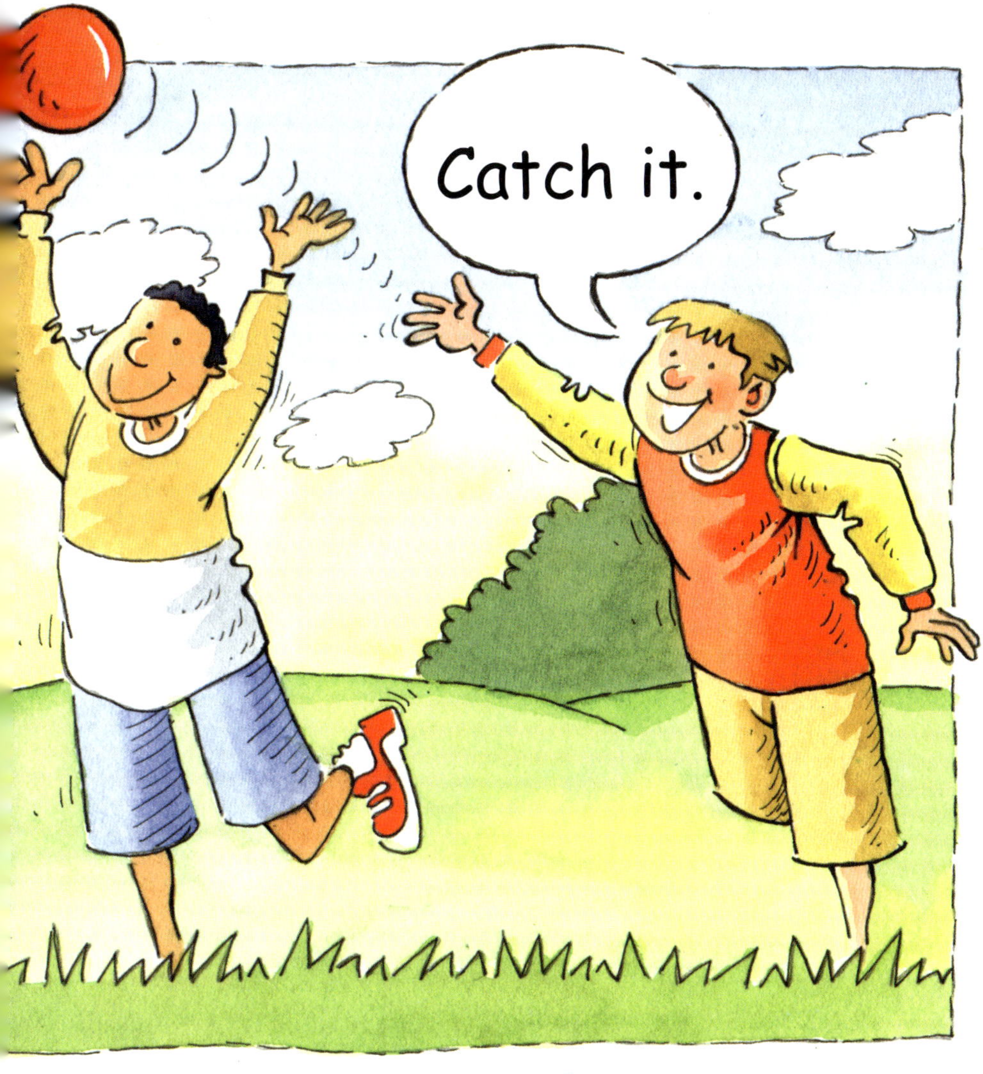
Catch it.

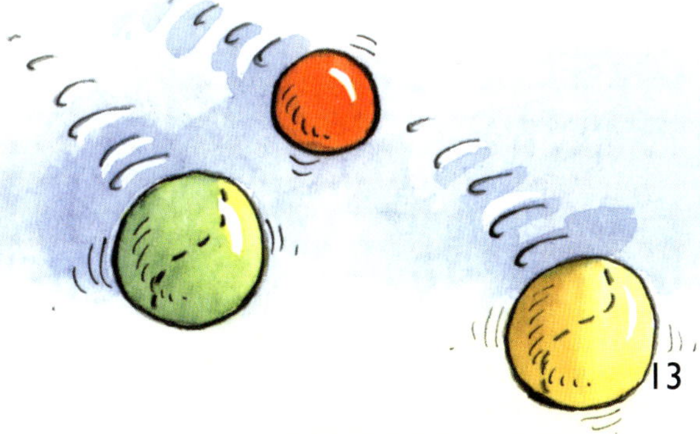

We like to roll balls.

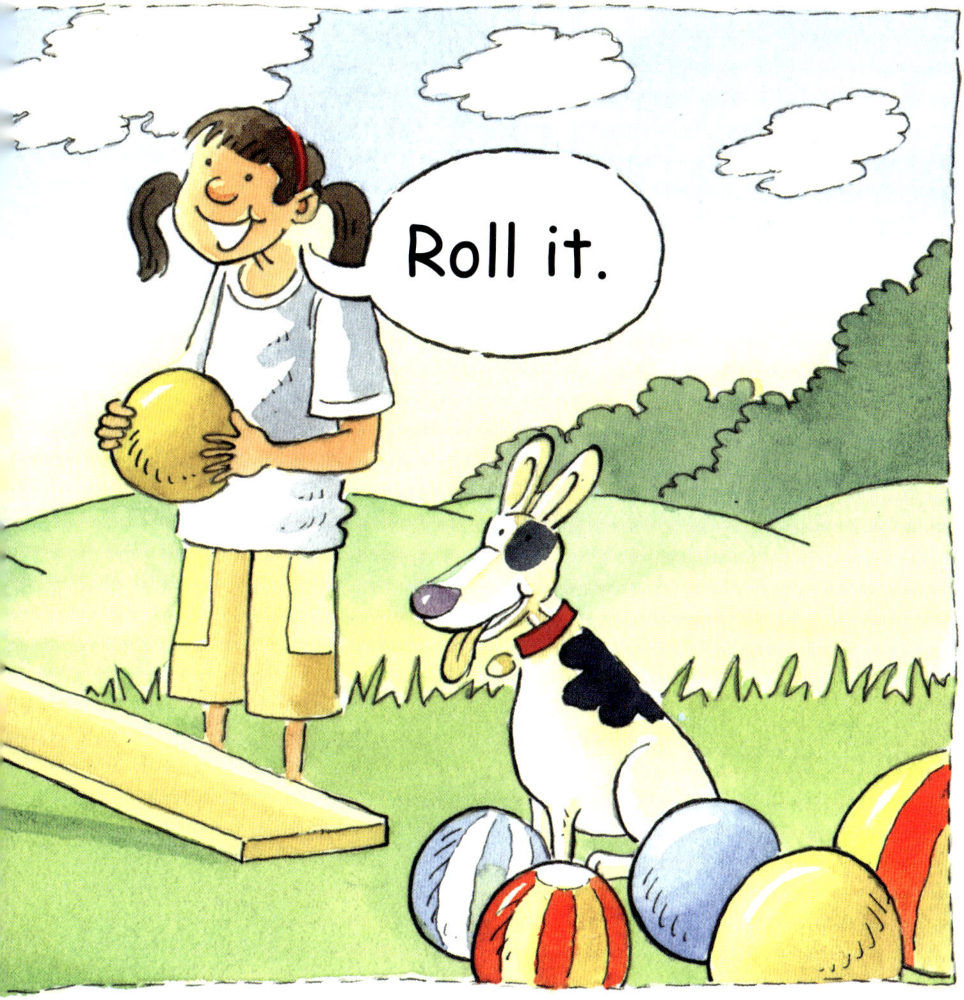
Roll it.

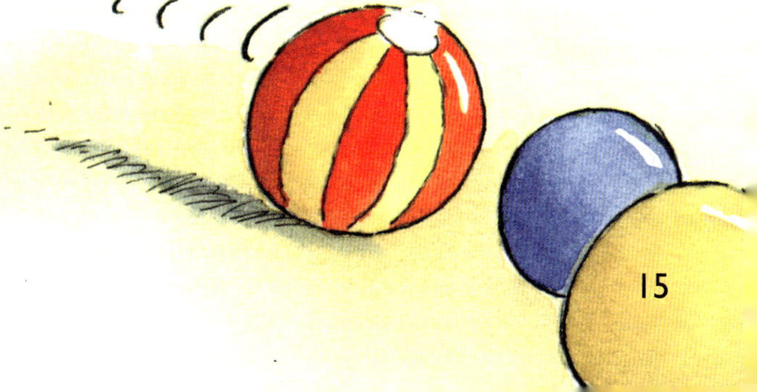

We like to juggle balls. Oooooops!